I HATE CHRISTMAS

ADVENT CALENDAR 2024

HOLIDAY CHEER? NOT HERE

© 2024 Jenna S. Rogers

All rights reserved. No part of this publication may be reproduced, distributed, or transmitted in any form or by any means, including photocopying, recording, or other electronic or mechanical methods, without the prior written permission of the publisher, except in the case of brief quotations embodied in critical reviews and certain other noncommercial uses permitted by copyright law.

Welcome to the 'I Hate Christmas' Advent Calendar

> **Snarky Quote:**
>
> "Holiday cheer?
> I'd rather have holiday peace and quiet."

Even though Christmas is meant to be the "most wonderful time of the year," let's face it: with all of the songs, shopping, family commitments, and pressure to be cheerful all the time, it can easily make you feel like the Grinch. And really, who can blame you? Congratulations! **You've discovered the perfect book if the idea of decorating the halls, feigning happiness for Secret Santa, or pretending to savor fruitcake makes you want to curl up until January.**

Here at the 'I Hate Christmas' Advent Calendar, we combine humor, sarcasm, and survival skills to help you get through the chaos. You can be found here rolling your eyes, sipping a Grinch drink, and taking peaceful pleasure in your Anti-Christmas Self-Care while everyone else is out there spreading holiday cheer.

This book is the perfect daily laugh, full of clever ideas and witty exercises to help you embrace your inner Scrooge and avoid stress. You'll discover a new method every day to parody, avoid, or at least get through the holidays. See it as an advent calendar with lots of opportunity to say "Nope" to the usual Christmas madness and lots of sarcasm instead of candy or adorable tiny gifts.

This book is intended to make the Christmas season a bit more bearable—and far more fun—whether you're avoiding gaudy sweaters, sending scathing letters to Santa, or coming up with absurd holiday customs that you'll never actually follow. Because, let's face it, sometimes the joy of the holidays lies in simply getting by.

So gather your favorite non-festive snack and your noise-canceling headphones, and let's begin a countdown of survival, sarcasm, and wit. **It's almost over, after all, and you merit a brief respite from the insanity of the holidays.**

How This Book Works

This advent calendar features a humorous quotation and an enjoyable holiday-themed activity every day to help you decompress, chuckle, or make light of the crazy times of the year. There will be days when you make goofy gift tags and days when you write more somber than cheerful letters to Santa. **However, you'll find enough of snark and a little humor every day to get you through the holiday season.**

Recall that the objective is to laugh at, avoid, and emerge from the pandemonium feeling as though you have won the fight of the holidays, not to embrace it.

Welcome to the 'I Hate Christmas' Advent Calendar. Let the sarcastic countdown begin. 🎄

1

Day 1: Christmas Survival Kickoff

> **Snarky Quote of the Day:**
>
> "Christmas spirit is in the air... or is that just panic?"

Greetings on the first day of the Advent Calendar "I Hate Christmas"!
Best wishes! You've survived the holiday season, a mystical time when the excitement of gift-giving gives way to the terror of navigating packed stores, hard-to-find merchandise, and never-ending lineups. All set to unleash your anti-holiday vibes? Now let's get started.

Activity:

List the top three things about Christmas shopping that irritate you. If you overdo it, you get bonus points. Go as farcical, theatrical, or ironic as you like! This is, after all, your time to let off steam.

To start using sarcasm, consider the following ideas:

The Crowds: "Well, I just adore interacting shoulder to shoulder with complete strangers who behave as though they have never seen a sale sign before. I can't get into the festive mood quite like a stampede at the checkout line!"

Music: "What's more enjoyable than listening to 'Jingle Bell Rock' for the forty-seventh time while searching for expensive socks?" Noise-canceling headphones are what I'm getting myself if I hear Mariah Carey just one more time."

The Presents: "Because there's no better way to say "I love you" than scrambling to find a gift that someone will pretend to like." Another gift card, oh my! Exactly what they've always desired, unless they have a secret detest

Now it's your turn!

Which three aspects of Christmas shopping are the most annoying for you? Put them in writing. Try to picture yourself conversing with someone who genuinely finds this insanity enjoyable. Make your grievances sound as though they belong in a Christmas soap opera. ("I almost lost my will to live because the lights in the mall were so blinding.")

1 ⬚

2 ⬚

3 ⬚

2

Day 2: Christmas Bullshit Bingo

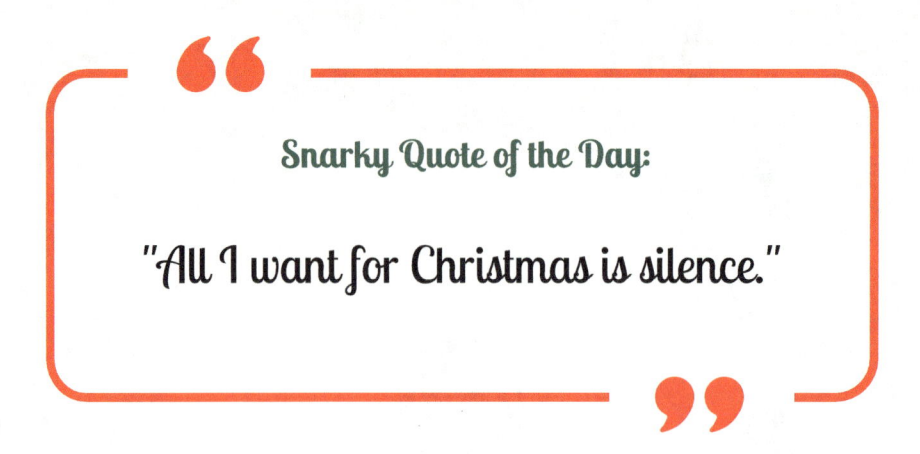

> **Snarky Quote of the Day:**
>
> "All I want for Christmas is silence."

Greetings on Day 2 of the Advent Calendar "I Hate Christmas"!

Congratulations! You've barely made it through Day 1. We're going to introduce you to a fun method to kill time this holiday season while also making fun of its silliness. Prepare for Christmas Bullshit Bingo, where you can mark squares whenever you see a cliché associated with the season in action. Let's make this chaos into a game!

Activity:

Win a Christmas Cliché Bingo game! Keep this bingo card close at hand throughout the Christmas season, and mark off any instances when you come across one of these clichés. Who knows? Maybe by midday, you'll prevail!

Instructions:

- Keep this bingo card in mind during your everyday holiday chaos.
- Whenever you spot one of these clichés in real life, mentally (or physically) cross it off.
- Share your victories with others—if you find someone else playing Christmas Bullshit Bingo, you've found a kindred spirit.

Bonus Challenge:

Check your speed at getting a "Bingo." When you finish a row, column, or diagonal, treat yourself to something unrelated to Christmas. Perhaps it's a pause for hot chocolate, but without the festive vibe.

Christmas Bullshit Bingo Card

Someone sings out-of-tune carols Your co-worker who thinks they're auditioning for "The Voice."	A mall Santa looks bored Bonus points if he's also on his phone.	An overpriced Christmas candle $50 for a candle that smells like pine trees? Sure... why not?	Someone gives a terrible gift Socks. Always socks.	Ugly Christmas sweater overload If you spot sequins, snowmen, and reindeer all at once—you win.
Burnt holiday cookies Grandma's cookies aren't quite the same when she forgets to set the timer.	"All I want for Christmas is you" plays Again. And again. And again.	Crowds fight over the last sale item Watch people battle over the last discounted blender.	Inflatable lawn decorations The bigger, the better, right? What's Christmas without a 20-foot snowman?	Christmas carolers They appear at the worst possible time... like when you're pretending not to be home.
Someone says "It's the most wonderful time of the year" As they look completely dead inside.	Forced office Secret Santa Because who doesn't love buying a gift for Karen in accounting?	Someone's outdoor Christmas lights blind you It's like looking directly into the sun.	Oversized turkey or ham Big enough to feed a small army, even though it's just your family of four.	Christmas tree falls over Bonus points if it happens during a party.
Late holiday cards You know, the ones that arrive in January... better late than never.	Power goes out from too many lights Too much Christmas spirit blew the breaker.	Last-minute gift wrapping disaster Tape in your hair, wrapping paper everywhere. Nailed it.	Family member gets tipsy at Christmas dinner And then the "fun" starts.	"Ho, ho, ho" overused We get it. You're festive. Now please stop.
Holiday work email with a festive GIF You can't escape the season, even in your inbox. Bonus if it's sparkly.	Someone dresses their pet in holiday gear Poor Fluffy didn't ask for that elf costume.	A holiday gift arrives damaged Just what you wanted—something broken. Merry Christmas!	Someone complains about gaining "holiday weight" Right before grabbing another cookie.	Fake snow decorations in a warm climate Nothing says "holiday spirit" like fake snow in 70-degree weather.

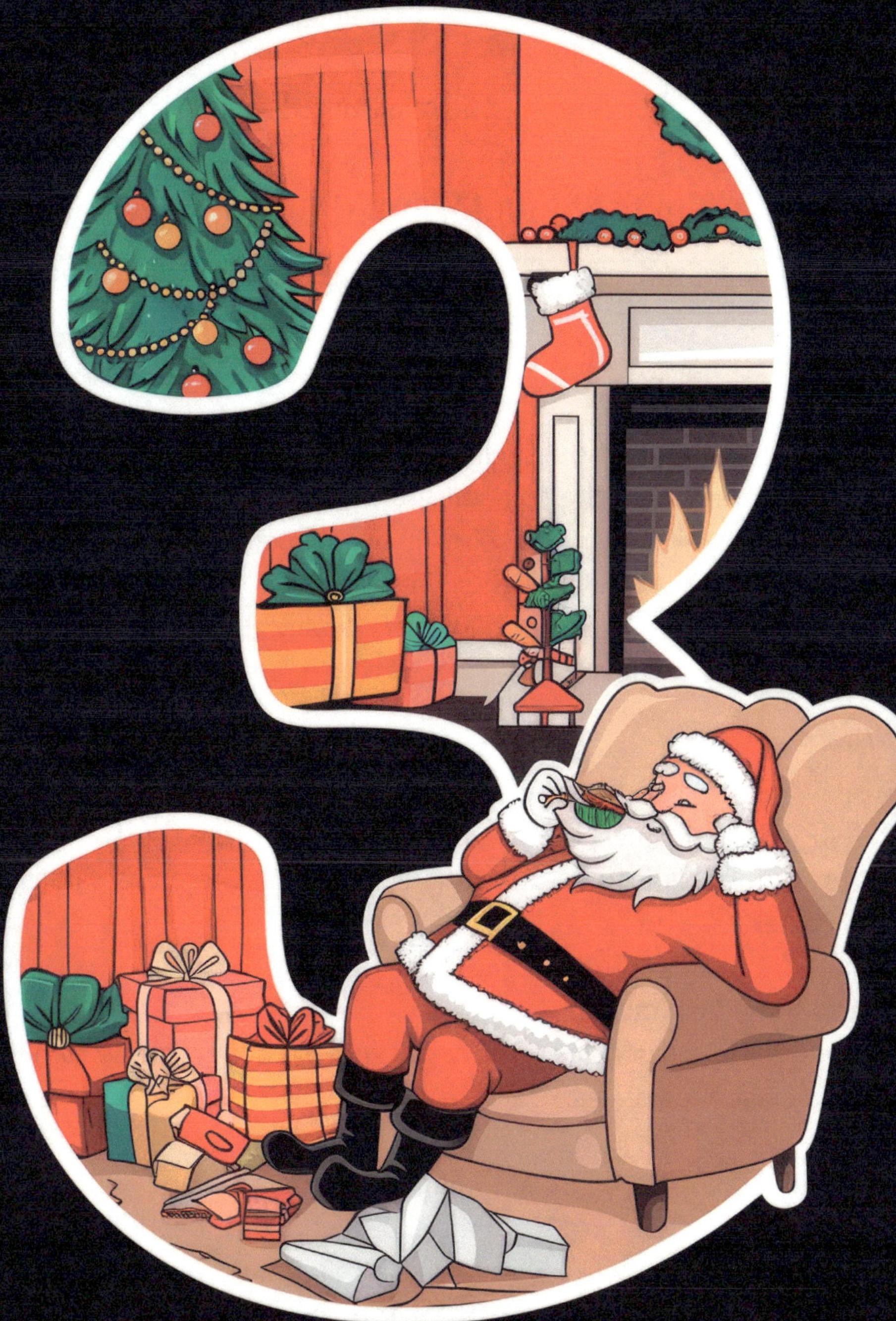

Day 3: Gratitude Journal (Sarcastic Edition)

> **Snarky Quote of the Day:**
>
> "I'm thankful for holiday traffic... said no one ever."

Welcome to Day 3 of the "I Hate Christmas" Advent Calendar!
It's time to embrace the spirit of gratitude... with a sarcastic twist, of course. While everyone else is busy being thankful for their cozy cocoa and twinkling lights, we're going to celebrate the little annoyances that make the holidays so "magical." Ready? Let's dive into your very own Sarcastic

Activity:

Today, your task is to write down the most irritating, frustrating, or downright annoying part of your day. **But here's the twist—you have to express it like you're thankful for it.** The more sarcastic, the better!

Need some inspiration?
Here are some examples of how to express your gratitude for life's holiday inconveniences:

Holiday Traffic: "I'm just SO thankful for the bumper-to-bumper traffic on my way to the mall today. Who needs to arrive anywhere on time when you have 45 minutes of quality 'me' time sitting in a car, inching forward at the speed of a distracted mall walker?"

Christmas Music Overload: "I'm so happy that 'Jingle Bells' came with me when I went from the grocery store to the coffee shop and back home. It's like having my very own happy soundtrack that never stops playing.

crowded stores: "Today in the checkout line, I felt extremely fortunate to have experienced such a wonderful moment with 25 strangers. The experience of waiting for the individual in front of us to search for precise change brought us all together.

Now it's your turn!

- Take a moment to think about the most annoying thing that happened today.
- Write it down as if it were the best thing to ever happen to you.
- Bonus points if you can imagine saying it out loud with a big, fake smile on your face.

4

Day 4: Bad Christmas Movie Marathon

> **Snarky Quote of the Day:**
>
> "Nothing like a terrible holiday movie to make you appreciate your life choices."

Greetings on Day 4 of the Advent Calendar "I Hate Christmas"! The ridiculous, corny holiday flicks that appear on your screen every December are something we've all seen. But let's embrace the ridiculousness and make it into a game rather than moaning every time one appears! It's time for the Bad Christmas Movie Marathon, where we sip hot chocolate and make fun of all the terrible holiday clichés.

Activity:

Settle back and chuckle at all the ridiculous moments in the cheesiest Christmas movie you can find (think small-town romances, too enthusiastic Santas, and much too much snow). Here's your task if you want to add even more intrigue:

Jot down any instance that seems ludicrous or impossible that you come across. Bonus points if you can predict the ending within the first 10 minutes.

Do you need assistance recognizing those movie cliches? Here are a few prominent instances of things to be cautious of:

Every Scene Contains Snow

"It's Christmas Eve, and for some reason, it hasn't stopped snowing for days, but nobody is shovelling their driveway. Unbelievable miraculous weather? Verify.

Quick Romance for the Holidays

"Oh, that's right! Within 48 hours, the attractive small-town baker and the powerful executive from the big metropolis fall in love. Completely credible. After just two dates, they are most definitely getting married.

Everything is Saved by Christmas

The local bakery was on the verge of closing, but surprisingly, Christmas magic came to the rescue! Who knew that the secret to success in business was cinnamon rolls?

Unachievably Ideal Families

"Observe that! The entire family was gathered around the tree, harmonizing their carols. No political disputes or passive-aggressive remarks regarding the origins of the mashed potatoes.

Abrupt Character Transformation

"After viewing glittering lights, the grouchy boss—who has detested Christmas for the past 25 years—had a change of heart. Yes, it is undoubtedly how emotional development occurs.

Bonus Game: Take a Hot Chocolate Shot!

Take a sip of hot chocolate—or whatever beverage you prefer—every time a character mentions the phrase "Christmas miracle." I promise that by the conclusion of these films, you'll be drenched in chocolate.

An example of a Log of Unrealistic Moments would be, *"Instead of doing mayor stuff, the small-town mayor spent half the movie hanging Christmas lights."*
"The streets covered in snow are immaculately clear, despite the fact that nobody uses shovels or plows."
"The main character walks through a snowstorm, and his hair looks amazing. Yes, exactly.

Extra Challenge: After the first ten minutes of the film, guess how it will conclude and check if you were correct. Warning: There's a chance you are.

So gather your blanket, settle in on the sofa, and indulge in the silliness. **Maybe you'll start to feel appreciative of the decisions you've made in life—at least you won't end up stuck attempting to rescue Christmas by competing with your ex in cookie baking!**

As you watch the film, keep in mind that things get better the worse they get.

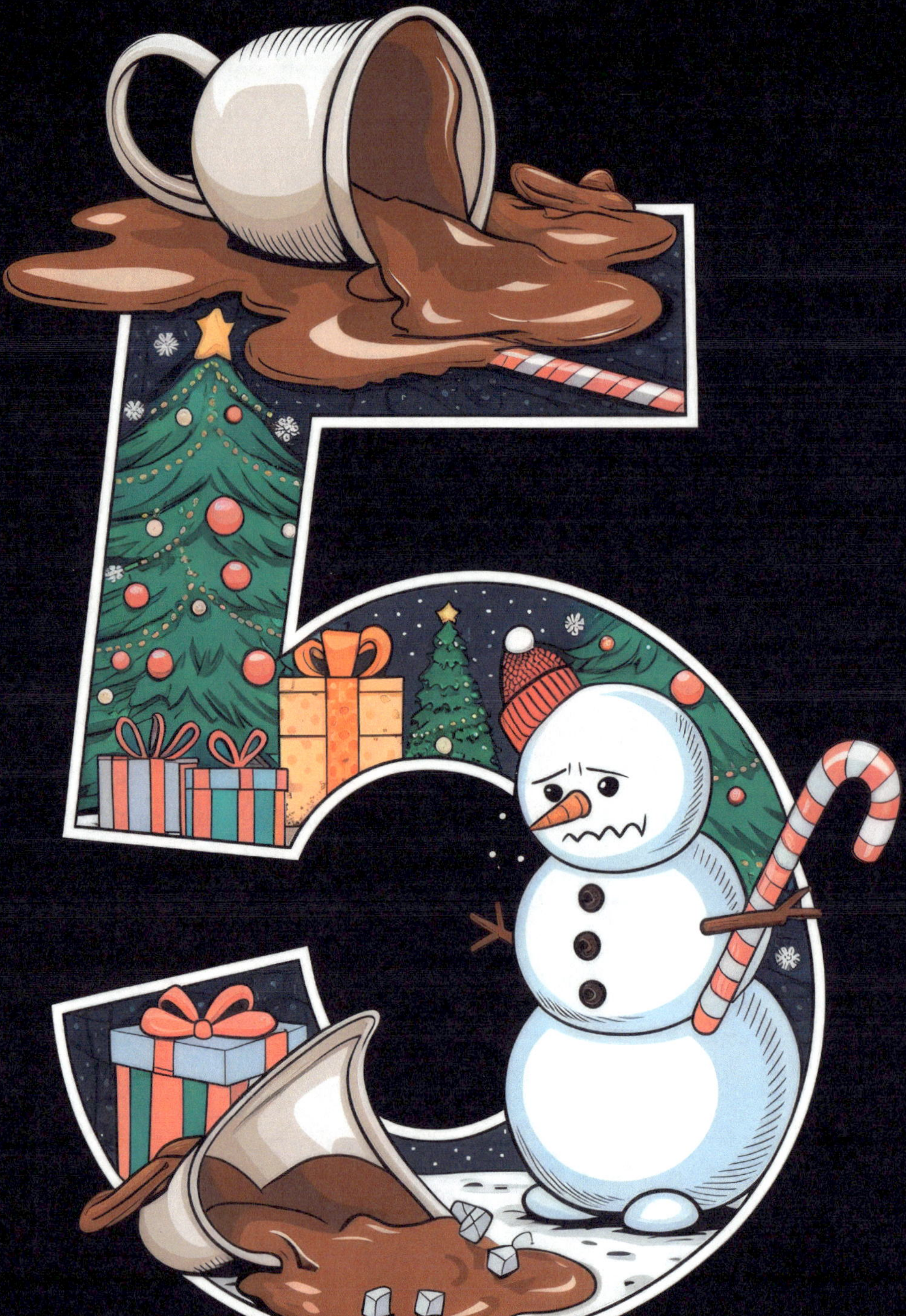

Day 5: Creative Stress-Relief Ideas

> **Snarky Quote of the Day:**
> "Who needs yoga when you can release stress by avoiding people and pretending Christmas doesn't exist?"

Greetings on Day 5 of the Advent Calendar "I Hate Christmas"! It's true that Christmas stress exists. However, rather than getting worked up over it, we're going to vent in some incredibly harmless and funny ways. Here, deep breathing and meditation are not necessary; instead, we're going to embrace witty, snarky ways to let go of our holiday frustration!

Activity:

Pick one of today's Innovative Stress-Relieving Ideas and do something really absurd to get your holiday sanity back. Choose your poison—er, I mean, your soothing pastime—from the possibilities available to you.

Activity: **Pick one of today's Innovative Stress-Relieving Ideas** and do something really absurd to get your holiday sanity back. Choose your poison—er, I mean, your soothing pastime—from the possibilities available to you.

Place crumpled receipts in a pretend fire

Gather all of the wrinkled receipts from all of your errands.

Now picture yourself in front of a raging fire (don't worry, it's just an imaginary fire; there are no fire safety risks involved).

Throw every receipt into the make-believe fires with a sense of drama. Say something like, "Goodbye, Christmas stress!" to add drama. I'll never understand you!

Observe how your stress is consumed by the mental fire. Please feel free to laugh uncontrollably if the spirit so pleases.

Bonus Challenge: You can increase the difficulty by adding the shattered wrapping paper remnants from your unsuccessful attempts to wrap gifts. More than twice as much pain as relief.

Include the flimsiest, most giddy praise in your Christmas card

Extract a blank holiday card (or simply a piece of paper; there's no reason to use an actual card for this).

Compose a Christmas card that is full of the most extravagant, ridiculous praises you can come up with. More fakery is preferable! For instance: "My life is made happier by your simple existence, Darling Karen, than by a thousand sparkling Christmas lights." Your cookies—oh, your cookies—are nothing short of divine intervention, and your festive attitude has the potential to melt the polar ice caps.

Give it your all. Make it seem as though this person is the only reason you are here, even when they are merely a coworker.

Bonus Challenge: Send this masterpiece by actual mail if you're feeling very sassy. Why not? Transmit some sardonic holiday cheer.

Stress-Relieving Snowball Warfare (Using Paper)

Gather some leftover paper (previous to-do lists work great for this) and roll it up into little balls called "snowballs."

Toss them at fictitious targets while standing across the room. Cheer for yourself each time you encounter a "imaginary holiday stressor" (such as the overpowering desire to purchase additional decorations or the pressure to throw the ideal party).

Simply respond to inquiries about your activities with, *"I'm winning at Christmas."* **since you are.**

Make the Most Passive-Aggressive Holiday Playlist in the World

Make yourself a playlist of holiday tunes that you enjoy, or that make you chuckle at how crazy the season can be. If you play songs like *"You're a Mean One, Mr. Grinch"* or *"Last Christmas"* for the thousandth time, you get bonus points.

Turn it up to full volume while you tidy up, wrap presents, or just sit there acting like you're interested.

Envision each note as a tiny release of your holiday stress. Or just use it to irritate your neighbors.

A humorous countdown to the holidays

Do you recall the paper chains you used to count down to Christmas when you were a child? Yes, that will return, albeit with a sardonic twist.

Write something witty about the holidays on each chain link. For instance, *"7 days until I smile through gritted teeth at Uncle Bob's jokes,"* or *"14 days until I fake enthusiasm for socks."*

Cut out one link each day leading up to Christmas. You'll be one step closer to making it through the season by the time it's all gone!

Extra Challenge: To relieve tension as much as possible, combine two or more activities. Who says you can't pretend to be praising your coworkers in a Christmas card and toss imaginary snowballs at them?

Recall that the objective is straightforward: survive the Christmas chaos without losing your sense of humor or sanity. Having fun and laughing at how ridiculous everything is is the main goals. So feel free to let rid of your tension in the funniest and most inventive way you can!

6

Day 6: Sarcastic Holiday Thank You Notes

> **Snarky Quote of the Day:**
>
> "Thanks for the sweater. Really. It's the perfect color... to re-gift."

Greetings on Day 6 of the Advent Calendar "I Hate Christmas"! Yes, the holidays are here again—the time of year when we get presents we didn't ask for, didn't want, and most likely won't use. But let's take a moment to express our gratitude—sarcastically, of course—instead of rolling our eyes and putting that ugly sweater in the back of your wardrobe!

Activity:

Compose **the world's sassiest thank-you card for a present** that you didn't like today. The idea is to come across as sincere and caring as you can, all the while slyly making fun of how much you actually don't enjoy it.

Do you need some motivation?

Here's how to write the ideal sarcastic note, complete with phony appreciation and excessive praise.

Begin with genuine courtesy (but not truly): *"Dear [present Giver], I am so grateful for the amazing [present you didn't ask for]. You really did beyond yourself this year!"*

As though it were the greatest thing ever, **provide a detailed description of the gift:** *"It's so amazing that you picked out this hideous sweater for me! It's really stunning, with its [questionable reindeer pattern] and [bright neon green]. It's unlike anything I've ever seen, and I doubt I ever will be.*

Put too much emphasis on what it "means" to you: *"I really don't know how I managed to get by for all these years without having such a... special item of apparel." I'm excited to wear this sweater to all the [invisible parties] I'll be attending this season because it's the ideal addition to my closet.*

Give a little backhanded compliment as well: *"I'm almost certain you have a second career as a professional gift selector because of how much consideration you've put into this gift. Could anyone else have suspected my covert desire for a [ceramic cat figurine]?*

Finish with an exuberant *"Once again, thank you for such a wonderful present. I have no doubt that it will provide me with countless joys. or, at minimum, offer some good prospects for regifting the next year. I hope you experience the same degree of kindness and care this holiday season!*

It's your turn now!
Consider a gift you've gotten that you weren't too delighted with, whether it was something from a hypothetical or previous Christmas.
Using the format mentioned above, compose a sarcastic thank-you note.
Bring out the best in you, pretending to be an award-winning actor or actress, but on the inside, you're secretly cringing.

Thank You

7

BAH HUMBUG

Day 7: Holiday Excuse Generator

> **Snarky Quote of the Day:**
>
> "I can't make it to the party. I have to alphabetize my spice rack."

Greetings on Day 7 of the Advent Calendar "I Hate Christmas"! Everybody has received the dreaded invitation to a Christmas party. Sometimes it's difficult to pretend to be excited for yet another holiday party, whether it's your neighbor's "Ugly Sweater Extravaganza" or your coworker's cookie exchange. But don't worry, you've found the ideal spot to create the ideal justification!

Activity:

Make a list of ridiculous but plausible justifications for skipping Christmas festivities today. These justifications ought to seem strange enough to ensure your escape while remaining plausible enough that nobody will doubt them. In order to be creative, think beyond the (present) box!

Do you need some motivation?
Here is a selection of pre-made justifications to get you going. You can make use of them or invent your own absurd justifications for avoiding the Christmas spirit.

List of absurd but believable excuses to get out of holiday parties

- "I would really like to come, but I'm stuck in a snowfall that's like a 500-piece puzzle right now. I have to maintain my momentum right now."

- "I'm still getting over last night's emotional rollercoaster of watching The Grinch." I need to digest the character development for at least a day."

- "This is the only chance I have to finally sort my socks by color alphabetically. I've been intending to do this for a while. You comprehend."

- "I'm having trouble getting my cat to sit still for holiday pictures. I'll have to work on it all evening."

- "I need to thank Santa for last year in writing. I don't want to be on the bad list, and it's long overdue."

- "I can't attend without my favorite ugly Christmas sweater, which I can't find. I would hate to let everyone down by not being really festive."

- "I have a workshop on how to get out of holiday parties, so I can't make it to the party." It's critical to my own development."

- "I've decided to abstain from social interaction while Mercury is retrograde. Believe me, it's for everyone's protection."

- "I'm only on the 1984 version of A Christmas Carol, but I've committed to binge-watching every version ever made, so I'd really love to be there. I have twelve left to do."

- "My fridge light went out, and I need to sit by it to make sure it doesn't come back on unexpectedly."

- "I have to concentrate since I'm getting ready for an amateur hot cocoa drinking competition. I can't allow the celebration get in the way of my training schedule."

- "I'm making sure nothing is missing by taking a close inventory of all my holiday decorations. It won't check itself, that false mistletoe."

- "I need to complete knitting my dog a humorous Christmas scarf. His Pomeranian dog breed is crucial to his vacation style."

Now it's your turn:

Now it's your turn!

- Think of a party you'd like to avoid.
- Create a list of absurd but totally believable excuses, just in case you need to make a quick exit.
- The more ridiculous, the better! After all, it's the holiday season—anything goes, right?

My list of absurd but believable excuses to get out of holiday parties

8

Day 8: DIY Anti-Christmas Cards

> **Snarky Quote of the Day:**
>
> *"Season's greetings... or not."*

Greetings on Day 8 of the Advent Calendar "I Hate Christmas"!
It's common knowledge that exchanging Christmas cards is a traditional aspect of the festive season. But why not add a sarcastic twist to the standard "Warmest Wishes" and "Merry and Bright" farewells? We're making DIY Anti-Christmas Cards today, which are ideal for expressing sentiments like "I care, but not that much."

Activity:

Create your own anti-Christmas card with a sarcastic message that appears happy but is actually meant to mislead no one. The message *"I care about you, but not enough to buy you something"* will be on today's card.

To add to the humor, pair the message with an extremely happy, festive design that exudes "holiday spirit" on the exterior while disclosing your actual emotions on the inside.

How to Make a Handmade Anti-Christmas Card

Select Your Media: If you're feeling low-tech, you can use actual paper and markers, a digital tool like Canva, or even a blank Word page. As long as you have a "card" to write on and decorate, anything will do.

The Front of the Card: Try to make the front look as extravagantly festive as you can. Consider use every holiday cliche you come across:

Design: Festive elves, candy canes, Santa's sleigh, snowflakes, and twinkling lights.

Message: Use a bright, glittery font and write something like "Wishing You All the Joy of the Season!" Make sure the appearance befits the contents.

The card's interior: This is the start of the real fun. Attempting to sound as "genuine" as possible, write this sarcastic remark inside the card: *"I care about you, but not enough to buy you something."*

To add even more sass, feel free to add any of the following:

"You're unique, but not $20 unique."
"I hope this card appeals to you. You are only going to receive it.
"This card is all I'm offering this year; it's basically a hug on paper."
Include a drawing inside:
Put a crazily happy doodle next to the message on the inside to really bring the humor home.

You may sketch an adorable little snowman who is very happy.
A reindeer dancing beneath a rainbow of twinkling Christmas lights, perhaps. **The trick is to keep the messaging delightfully snarky while making the drawing as happy as possible.**

9

HO
HO
NO

Day 9: Fun Fact You Didn't Ask For

> **Snarky Quote of the Day:**
>
> *"Did you know? Christmas used to be illegal in Massachusetts!"*

Greetings on Day 9 of the Advent Calendar "I Hate Christmas"! Who doesn't enjoy a strange historical fact that challenges preconceived notions about the holidays? This is a really easy exercise for today, but it will definitely make you laugh and potentially confuse your friends. You're going to discover a weird, unusual Christmas truth, consider how ridiculous it is, and then impart this merry information to someone who wasn't prepared for it. Sincerely, why not?

Activity:

You'll learn a strange Christmas fact today that will leave you wondering how the holidays came to be so... well, strange. Let's explore one of the most bizarre incidents in the history of Christmas.

Daily Fun Fact: Were you aware of this? In the past, Massachusetts did not allow Christmas!

That is correct, really. Christmas celebrations were outlawed in Massachusetts from 1659 to 1681.

Christmas was too closely associated with pagan customs and too boisterous for the Puritans, who took their religious convictions and abstinence from pleasure extremely seriously. Thus, a legislation prohibiting celebrations was passed. Five shillings could be fined to anyone found rejoicing!

That would be like receiving a fine for excessively celebrating the holidays! These days, if half the nation put up Christmas decorations before Thanksgiving, they probably would have to arrest people for it.

Activity:

Step 1: Read this interesting information and ponder for a moment on how ridiculous it is. Try not to chuckle too much when you consider the contemporary counterpart (such as getting arrested for repeatedly playing "All I Want for Christmas" by Mariah Carey).

Step 2: Tell someone today about this strange information. It can be a stranger, a friend, or a coworker who appears to be in need of some unusual holiday facts.

Step 3: Observe their expression as they come to terms with the fact that Christmas, the world's most extravagant festival, was once prohibited. Points awarded if they inquire, "Wait... seriously?"

How to Communicate This Information:

In Person: Bring up this fact in casual conversation. Say something like, *"Did you know that Christmas used to be illegal in Massachusetts?"* while talking about your holiday plans. It gives me all the justification I need to despise it.

"Hey, random question: Did you know that Christmas was illegal in Massachusetts in the 1600s?" was sent by text message. The Grinches originated with the Puritans.

Regarding Social Media:

Share a message along the lines of, *"If you think your family's Christmas traditions are rigorous, try living in Massachusetts in the 1600s, when Christmas was truly forbidden."* That's enjoyable, then.

Extra Fun Fact Challenge: After sharing the odd Christmas fact of the day, find another odd holiday custom or piece of historical information. The world of Christmas is full with ridiculous things! items like the Yule Cat—an Icelandic folklore creature that devours people who don't receive new clothes for Christmas—or the peculiar Japanese custom of having KFC for Christmas supper are items you might come across.

It's your turn now!

Talk about the strangeness and observe the bewildered looks that follow. Who knows? Perhaps you'll establish a new custom of disseminating interesting knowledge rather than holiday happiness!

And never forget to remind them that Christmas was once outlawed when life provides you excessive holiday celebrations. That will undoubtedly provoke thought.

10

Day 10: Holiday Countdown Checklist (the Real Version)

> **Snarky Quote of the Day:**
>
> *"Only 15 more days of avoiding people!"*

Greetings on Day 10 of the Advent Calendar "I Hate Christmas"!
It's a reason for pride that you've come this far. However, we're going against the grain and not counting down to all the joyful silliness. Making a holiday countdown checklist is today's task—but not the kind where you make a to-do list. Oh no, we're celebrating the things you're trying so hard to avoid today. Think of it as your own personal defense plan for the holidays!

Activity:

Compile a list of all the traditions, events, and activities connected to the holidays that you have managed to avoid or that you have decided to forego this year. You'll feel proud of yourself, I promise, even for staying out of the chaos. It's time to master the skill of refusing the chaos of the holidays!

Do You Need Some Motivation?
To help you get started on everything you could be steering clear of this season, here is a checklist. Please feel free to contribute your own nightmares to the list!

The Complete Holiday Avoidance Guide

Mall Holiday Shopping

"This year, I avoided the crowded mall—many thanks to internet shopping! No fighting in the parking lot, no never-ending lineups, and no lugging a cart through mayhem while blasting "Jingle Bells" on repeat."

Going to a Holiday Party at Work

"Oh no, I'm not able to participate in this year's Secret Santa gift exchange. I'm quite busy with everything else right now."

Joining the neighbors in caroling

I apologize, but I will not be able to sing uncomfortably in front of strangers and pretend that I enjoy it. I cannot sing "silent night" or any other night in my vocal range."

Decorating every square inch of the home

"This year, I skipped the extravagant decorating. Thank you, the single depressing strand of lights on my front porch is festive enough."

Making Christmas Cookie Baking

I'm so relieved that I didn't bake a single batch of cookies this year. It feels good to keep the kitchen free of sugar-induced meltdowns and flour explosions."

The Contest for Ugly Sweaters

Wearing anything that appears to have been created by a colorblind elf is strongly discouraged. I'll be comfortable in my go-to sweater, please."

Present-Wrapping with a Pinterest-Grade Adoration

"I finished off the day by wrapping everything in simple brown paper and taping it shut. Nothing Instagram-worthy will be wrapped as gifts here."

Seeing Every Overrated Christmas Film

"I succeeded in avoiding the required holiday movie marathon of corny flicks. Not a single romantic comedy to be found. Are I a hero in my heart? Perhaps.

Christmas Cards

"I escaped the whole Christmas card debacle. No snapping pictures, no handwritten notes, no card-giving. I don't need to post one more photo of myself clumsily clutching a cocoa mug to the internet."

Stopping by Santa at the Mall

"I don't think I'll wait an hour in line to sit on someone else's lap. I'm fine, Santa can have his candy cane.

Putting up a Holiday Meal

"Skipped the anxiety of preparing a feast and striking up conversation with far-off relatives at a dinner party. It's pizza, baby!"

Jokes about the Elf on the Shelf

"I was able to refrain from creating absurd elf scenarios throughout the house. This year, my living room won't have a tiny elf zip-lining over it."

Taking Part in Exchanges of Gifts

"No, I didn't take part in the sharing of "White Elephant" gifts. I reasoned that this year, we could all use one fewer pointless gift."

Christmas Crafts

Successfully steered clear of any glitter-related DIY Christmas crafts. The true gift is that my house will continue to be devoid of sparkle."

Now It's Your Turn!

Take a few minutes to create your own Holiday Avoidance Checklist. What have you dodged so far? What will you proudly avoid in the days ahead?

Remember, this is all about self-care and preserving your sanity, so feel free to celebrate the things you're not doing.
Write your list, smile to yourself, and bask in the glory of saying "no" to holiday madness.

Bonus Challenge:
After creating your list, share it with a fellow holiday-hater. Maybe you'll inspire them to start their own avoidance checklist. The less, the merrier!

My Holiday Avoidance Checklist

- [ ] _____
- [ ] _____
- [ ] _____
- [ ] _____
- [ ] _____
- [ ] _____
- [ ] _____
- [ ] _____
- [ ] _____
- [ ] _____
- [ ] _____
- [ ] _____
- [ ] _____

11

CHRISTMAS IS OVERRATED.

Day 11: Grinch Mode Self-Assessment

> **Snarky Quote of the Day:**
>
> "On a scale of one to full Grinch, how over it are you?"

Greetings on Day 11 of the Advent Calendar "I Hate Christmas"!
A Grinch Mode Self-Assessment is in order. To be honest, not everyone enjoys hot chocolate over the holidays. You may have a brief holiday mood on certain days, but on others you'll be itching to steal the roast beast and hide in your mountain cave.

The goal of today's exercise is to determine your exact level of holiday fatigue. Have you gone completely Grinch mode, or are you just a little irritated? Let's investigate!

Activity:

On a scale of 1 to 10, indicate how festive you are feeling right now. After that, spend some time writing in your journal on what's preventing you from becoming the amazing "full Grinch." Prepare to embrace your holiday humbug and give way to your inner Grinch.

Grinch Mode Scale

Grinch Mode Level	Description
1	"I'm shockingly jolly today. What's happening to me?"
2	"I smiled at a holiday decoration… but don't tell anyone."
3	"The cookies smell nice, but I'm still not impressed."
4	"I might hum a carol, but it's purely accidental."
5	"Half Grinch, half human. Festive, but with a side of sass."
6	"I rolled my eyes at someone saying 'Merry Christmas.'"
7	"I would rather listen to nails on a chalkboard than more carols."
8	"I'm fantasizing about hiding every single ornament in the house."
9	"I have a plan to steal all the Christmas trees on my street."
10	"I *am* the Grinch. The holidays can't end soon enough."

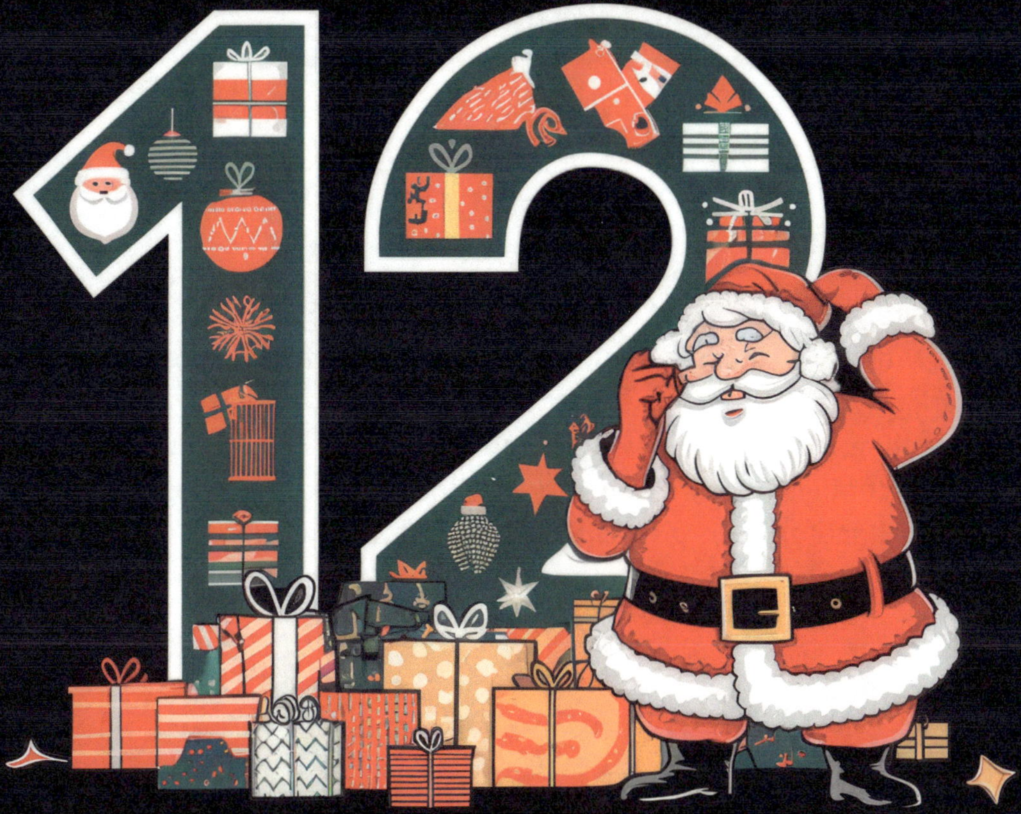

Day 12: Anti-Gift Ideas

> **Snarky Quote of the Day:**
>
> *"The best gift is no gift."*

Greetings on Day 12 of the Advent Calendar "I Hate Christmas"! Now that we've passed halfway through, it's time to start thinking seriously about holiday shopping. Instead of worrying about selecting meaningful gifts, why not just enjoy the satisfaction of giving nothing at all? The task for today is to compile a list of absurd anti-gifts, or gifts that proclaim, "I thought about you... for exactly five seconds."

Activity:

Make a list of absurd presents you would like to give. The more ridiculous and effortless the better! If you could provide things that no one requested or desired, just think of it. This is your opportunity to adopt a sardonic, anti-gifting stance.

Do you need some motivation?
Here is a selection of absurd anti-gifts to spark your imagination. Please feel free to make use of these suggestions or devise your own incredibly awful gifts!

Fake Anti-Gift Ideas

A Jar of Nothing

Because nothing says 'I care' quite like a jar that is empty. Put air in it and refer to it as a "fresh holiday breeze."

A "One Free Day of Silence" coupon

"The ideal present for someone who talks too much. Redeemable without my presence.

"Do Not Disturb Sign"

For those who always manage to track you out when you're attempting to hide, a "Do Not Disturb" sign. You may now officially make it official with a door sign.

Just One Sock

Just one sock. Just one, not two. It represents my feelings on holiday shopping, which are jumbled and incomplete.

A Defunct Gift Card

"This $50 gift card was meant to expire last year. I apologize! Isn't it true that the notion itself matters?

A Tailored To-Do List

"I wrote a list of the things I would really like you to do for me. Please begin as soon as the holidays are over.

An Unused Coupon "Coupon Book" Made by Hand

You have rights to stuff like "One Free High Five," "Permission to Text Me Later," and "A Compliment When I Feel Like It" if you read this book. Though it's essentially useless, have fun!

A "Happy Birthday! "You've Survived the Holidays" certificate

"Because barely making it through the season says success." Put it in perspective. Flaunt your passable achievement.

Just One Tube of Wrapping Paper

"I kept the tube from the wrapping paper for you." Thank you very much. Now, it's a flexible stick made of cardboard.

The Perfect Re-Gift: Something You Acquired Previous Year

"Last Christmas, I received this candle. Now that I haven't utilized it, it is yours! Is there anything more joyous than reusing gifts?

A "You Tried" Post-It note Inscribed on It

Put it somewhere to serve as a constant reminder that you tried. For modest expectations, it's the ideal gift.

A Sack of Remaining Wrapping Paper

"This bag of miscellaneous leftover paper scraps is for the crafty person. Take pleasure in assembling something unsightly.

A fork made of plastic

"Because, let's not get carried away, silverware is always helpful. You should be able to finish at least one meal using one plastic fork.

A VIP Ticket to Nothing

You currently have zero "exclusive access" to anything. You are welcome to use this somewhere that it isn't accepted.

The "Good Vibes" Gift

"From a distance, I'm sending you positive energy. No tangible gift is required. Imagine the vibes, please.

A Customized Spotify Playlist with Music I Enjoy (Not You)

"My favorite songs are on this playlist, not yours. You either adore it or detest it. In any case, you're welcome.

An Entire Mason Jar of My "Holiday Cheer"

"It's empty because, well, I'm not really feeling festive. But isn't the jar adorable?

It's Your Turn Now!
Create a list of absurd goods that you would love to give as presents for the holidays.

Be as inventive (or indolent) as you choose. The idea is to design gifts that, despite their humorous lack of utility, manage to evoke the joy of the holidays in you.

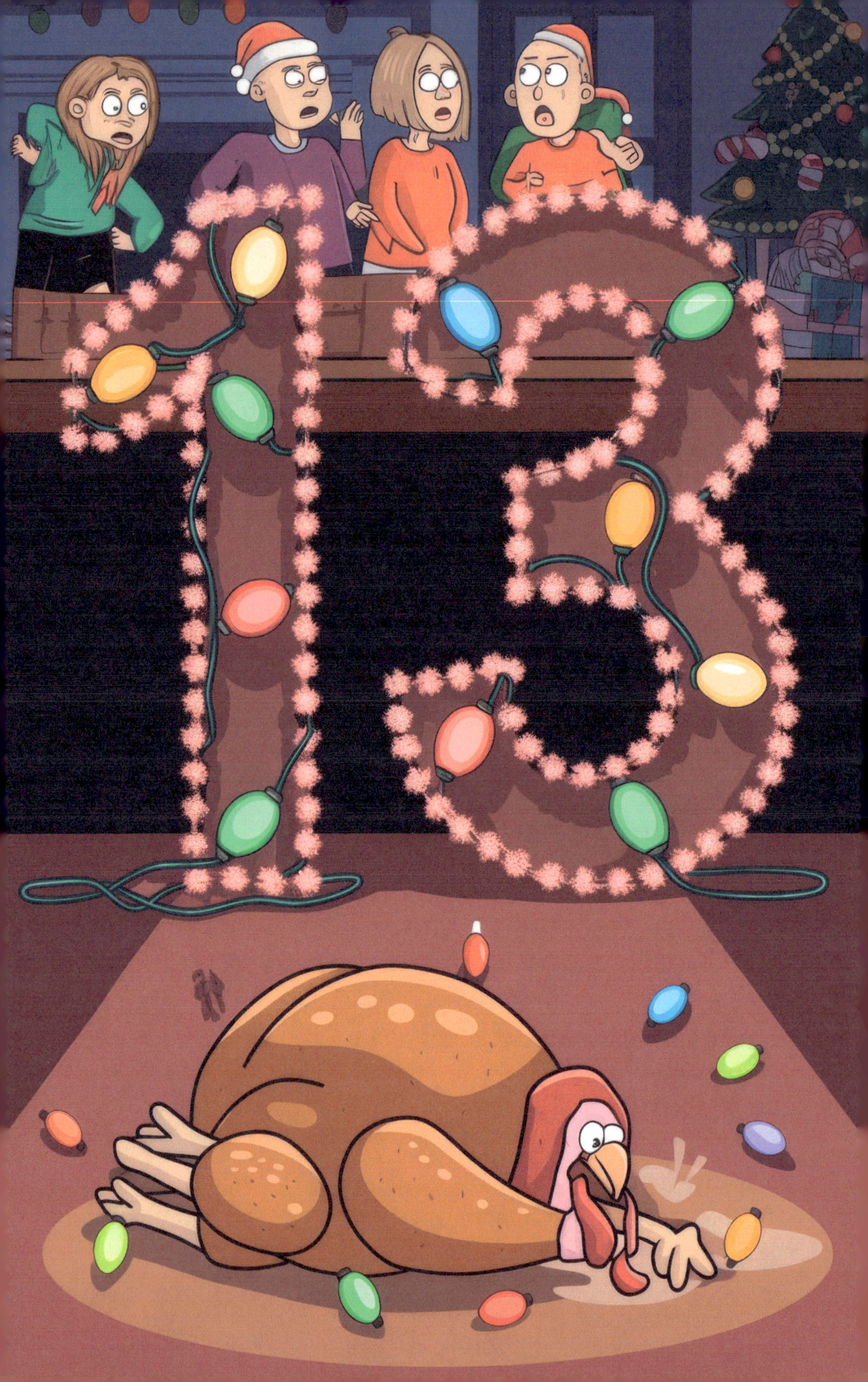
13

Day 13: Sarcastic Christmas Scenarios

> **Snarky Quote of the Day:**
>
> "Christmas is magical...
> if by magical you mean stressful."

Greetings on Day 13 of the Advent Calendar "I Hate Christmas"!
What could be more enjoyable than imagining the ideal vacation? Of course, imagining the opposite sarcastically! Filling in sarcastic Christmas scenarios is the focus of today's exercise, which allows you to lightheartedly express your outrage at the absurdity of the holiday. Since nothing quite embodies "holiday cheer" like making fun of everything that goes wrong.

Activity:

Finish the mocking scenarios with a festive theme below. Use your most ridiculous, indolent, or extravagant ideas to fill in the blanks. The more absurd your responses are, the better! This is your opportunity to make light of the mayhem that is Christmas and how things never quite turn out the way you planned.

Sarcastic Christmas scenarios

"I'll get .... (adjective) socks instead of what I want for Christmas, which is .... (noun)."
For instance: "All I want for Christmas is a private island, but instead, I'll get itchy socks."

"It's not Christmas until someone .... (verb) the tree and knocks over .... (noun)."
For instance: "It's not Christmas until someone tackles the tree and knocks over Aunt Susan's 50-year-old snow globe collection."

"The only thing better than holiday shopping is .... (verb) through a crowd of .... (plural noun) while listening to .... (annoying holiday song) on repeat."
For instance: "The only thing better than holiday shopping is elbowing through a crowd of screaming toddlers while listening to "Feliz Navidad" on repeat."

"This year, I'm hoping to avoid .... (holiday-related disaster), but knowing my luck, I'll end up .... (verb) instead."
For instance: "This year, I'm hoping to avoid burning the turkey, but knowing my luck, I'll end up setting off the smoke alarm instead."

"My idea of holiday relaxation is ....(verb) in front of the fireplace while .... (relative) asks me for the 10th time if I'm ....(question you hate)."
For instance: "My idea of holiday relaxation is pretending to nap in front of the fireplace while Uncle Bob asks me for the 10th time if I'm still single."

"I'm going to .... (dramatic action) if I have to hear .... (holiday song) one more time. However, there is at least .... (noun) to keep me sane."

For instance: "I'm going to launch myself into space if I have to hear "All I Want for Christmas Is You" one more time. However, drinking helps to keep me sane at least."

"All I want for Christmas is .... (noun), but instead I'll get stuck .... (verb) with .... (person)."

For instance: "All I want for Christmas is peace and quiet, but instead I'll get stuck wrapping presents with my chatty cousin."

It's Your Turn Now!

Complete each sarcastic holiday scenario with your own outrageous, hilarious suggestions.

This is your moment to let out all of your humorous holiday tension, so don't hold back.

Bonus Task: Give your finished scenarios to a relative or acquaintance who could use a good laugh. Maybe you two should make it a holiday tradition to complete sarcastic scenario books!

Don't forget that Christmas is enchanting. but only if tension, awkward small conversation, and excessive amounts of glitter are part of your notion of magic. Laugh your way through it, please!

14

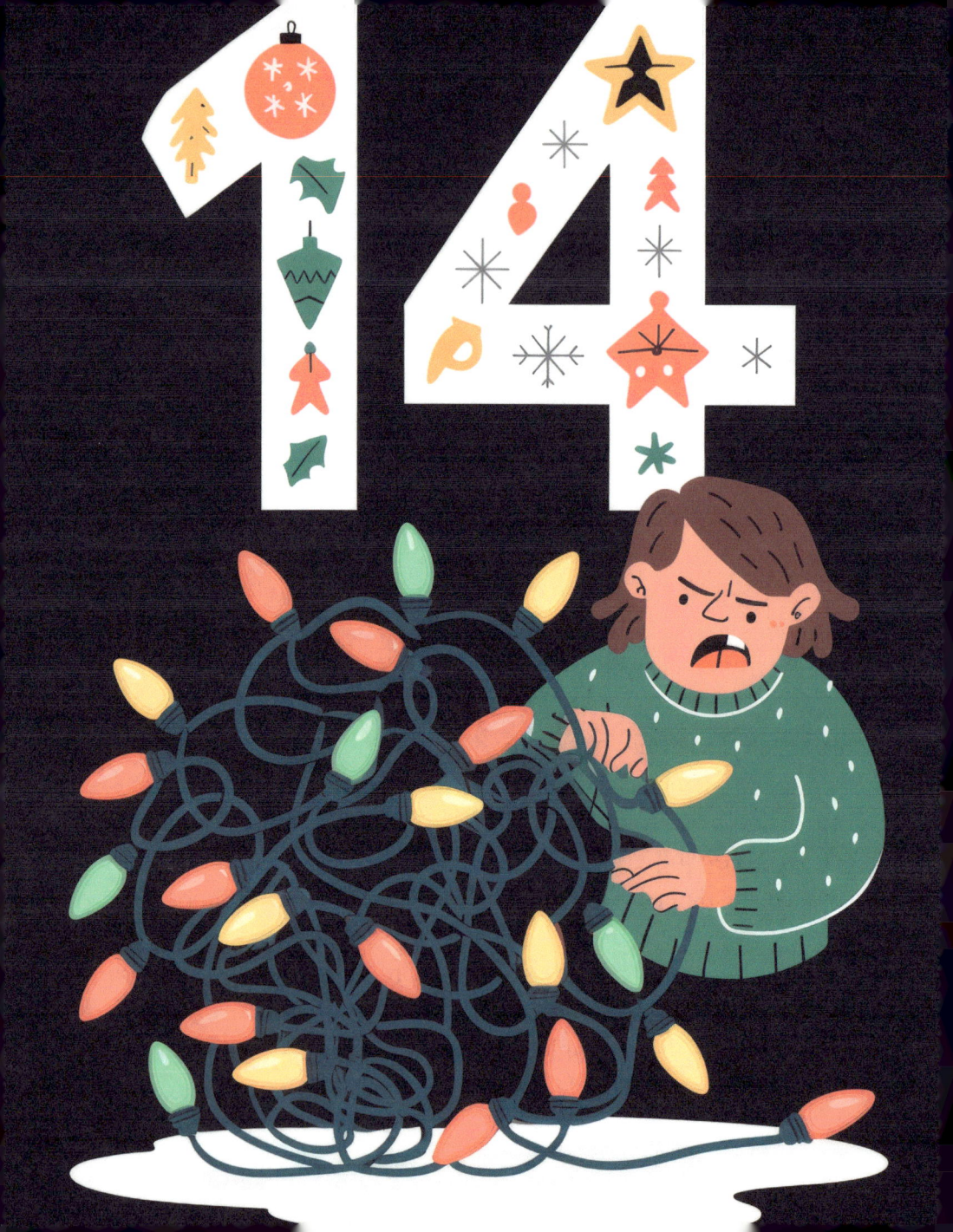

Day 14: Anti-Christmas Carols

> **Snarky Quote of the Day:**
>
> "I'd rather listen to nails on a chalkboard than more carols."

Greetings on Day 14 of the Advent Calendar "I Hate Christmas"! Since November, Christmas carols have been playing nonstop, to the point where even the most upbeat song can become unbearable. Don't give up though, because you can release your holiday angst by recreating popular Christmas songs with a caustic, anti-Christmas twist in today's exercise. Prepare to transform "Jingle Bells" into "Shopping Hells" and "Silent Night" into "Stressful Night"!

Activity:

Select a well-known Christmas song and alter the lyrics to express your true feelings about the occasion. You can be as nasty as you want to be—this is your time to turn those joyous carols on their head!

Do you need some motivation?
To get you started, consider these anti-Christmas renditions of some beloved carols:

Original: "Silent Night"
Anti-Christmas Version: "Stressful Night"
Tune: Silent Night

Stressful night,
Shopping fright,
Presents due, no money in sight.
Piles of wrapping, nothing goes right,
Eating cookies well past midnight,
Christmas can't end soon enough,
Christmas can't end soon enough.

Original: "Jingle Bells"
Anti-Christmas Version: "Shopping Hells"
Tune: Jingle Bells

Dashing through the store,
In a frantic, stressed-out way,
Through the crowds I soar,
Trying to survive the day.
Bells on cashiers ring,
Prices make me cry,
Oh what fun it is to scream,
When your credit card gets denied!

Chorus:
Shopping hells, shopping hells,
Why is it this way?
Oh what fun it is to fight
For deals on Christmas Day, hey!
Shopping hells, shopping hells,
I'll just stay inside,
This holiday is way too much,
I think I'll run and hide.

Original: "We Wish You a Merry Christmas"
Anti-Christmas Version: "We Wish You a Quiet Christmas"
Tune: We Wish You a Merry Christmas

We wish you a quiet Christmas,
We wish you a quiet Christmas,
We wish you a quiet Christmas,
And an even quieter New Year!
No more carols, no more cheer,
Just peace and quiet all year.
We wish you a quiet Christmas,
And maybe a long nap, too.

Original: "Deck the Halls"
Anti-Christmas Version: "Wreck the Halls"
Tune: Deck the Halls

Wreck the halls with stress and chaos,
Fa la la la la, la la la la!
Christmas cheer? I think I'll pass,
Fa la la la la, la la la la!
Tangle up the Christmas lights,
Fa la la, la la la, la la la!
Everything's a losing fight,
Fa la la la la, la la la la!

Now It's Your Turn!
- Choose your least favorite (or most overplayed) Christmas song.
- Rewrite the lyrics with an anti-Christmas twist.
- Feel free to get creative—whether it's complaining about endless shopping, awkward family gatherings, or the sheer exhaustion of holiday prep, this is your chance to have fun with it!

15

Day 15: Sarcastic Santa Letter

> **Snarky Quote of the Day:**
>
> *"Dear Santa, all I want is peace and quiet."*

Greetings on Day 15 of the Advent Calendar "I Hate Christmas"! It's time for Santa to get genuine. All you're doing is attempting to make it through the season without losing your sanity, while everyone else is busy demanding expensive toys and devices. The goal of today's exercise is to write a sarcastic letter to Santa. In it, you can make genuine holiday desires, such as getting people to stop talking about their holiday shopping or building a robot that can wrap gifts to save you from sticky tape mishaps.

Activity:

Compose a sardonic letter to Santa Claus requesting useful, cost-effective gifts that you genuinely require this year. This is your chance to get creative and let the big guy in red know what you need, whether it's a personal bubble to avoid social situations or a mute button for all Christmas music.

Do you need some motivation?
Here's an example of a satirical letter to get you going:

Dear Santa,

I hope you are doing well, or at least faring better than I am, as the holidays are already stressing me out. Though I understand that you're preoccupied getting ready for your special night, I thought I'd make a few requests. I'm not asking for anything extremely complicated, so don't worry. Just a few useful items to help me get through this season of "joyous."

To begin with, is it possible to stop everyone from discussing their holiday shopping? I understand. Everybody needs to purchase gifts. But I'm going to start wrapping empty boxes for fun if I have to hear about one more Black Friday sale.

It would be fantastic if you could also bring me a robot that wraps presents. Attempting to cut straight lines with wrapping paper has taken up more of my time than actually purchasing gifts. I have three rolls of wrapping paper missing from a closet I'm afraid to access, and my fingers are taped together.

And, Santa, could you please create a personal mute button while you're at it? In particular, for all the Christmas carols that are continuously playing in every store.

Let's also discuss holiday get-togethers. Is there any way you could make me an invisibility cloak? I wish I could miss a couple of things without anyone noticing. Better yet, perhaps you could bestow upon me the ability to make up acceptable explanations for myself that don't require me to lie about having the "mysterious flu."

Regards, Santa. Since you're probably busy,

I hope you're making it through the holidays,
[Name]

Dear Santa,

16

Day 16: DIY Holiday Escape Plan

> **Snarky Quote of the Day:**
>
> *"You can't escape Christmas... or can you?"*

Greetings on Day 16 of the Advent Calendar "I Hate Christmas"!
It's true that over the holidays, there can be too much going on. You may want to run away from it all, what with the nonstop carols, hectic shopping, and incessant forced smiles. You're going to organize your dream vacation from everything festive today—your ultimate Christmas hideaway. Who says you can't vanish for the holidays, after all?

Activity:

Where in the world would you go if you could disappear and avoid the holidays? Put it in writing and see yourself there, distant from the never-ending cycle of holiday commitments and "Jingle Bells." Today is all about planning the ideal vacation, whether it's on a tropical island or in a remote lodge in the mountains.

Do you need some ideas to help you get away?
To get you going, here are some ideal locations and circumstances:

Option 1: A Tropical Island Hideout

I mean, when you're drinking from a coconut while relaxing on the beach, "Merry Christmas" sounds a lot less stressful.
Where: On a private island in the South Pacific, the sound of the waves gently lapping on the shore is all that can be heard. Nothing to decorate for the holidays, no Christmas lights—just total relaxation.
What's Going to Happen: Rather than carolers, wake up to the sound of the waves.
Linger in a hammock all day reading a book that has nothing to do with the holidays.
Drink fruity drinks that have tiny umbrellas in them and stay away from eggnog that has been spiked.
Make sandcastles rather than gingerbread homes.
Watch the sun fall over the horizon and forget Christmas ever happened.

Option 2: Cozy Mountain Cabin (No Wi-Fi)

This is the ideal retreat for those times when you just want to cuddle up with a blanket and shut out the outside world.
Where: A little, remote lodge surrounded by snow-covered trees in the mountains, far from the bustle of the holidays.
What's Going to Happen: Get comfortable with a stack of non-Christmas films and light a fire.
Without any marshmallows with festive themes, sip hot chocolate.
Take some time to enjoy the snowfall without feeling compelled to make a snowman.
Savor the quiet—no Christmas carols, no jingles, no "Ho Ho Ho." You alone with the sounds of nature.
Unplug entirely; that means no Christmas emails, last-minute gift shopping, or invitations to ugly sweater parties if there is no Wi-Fi.

Option 3: Traveling by car to nothing

Desire to truly escape? Get in your vehicle and go until the Christmas lights are no longer visible in your rearview mirror.
Where: Outside of this place. Nothing to look forward to, just an open road, a full gas tank, and the ability to drive till you find silence.
What's Going to Happen: Play a playlist devoid of any Christmas tunes at all.
Make a few stops at unplanned restaurants and lodging establishments that lack holiday décor (it's a hard find, but you'll get it).
Explore fresh locales that are immune to the chaos of the holidays.
Savor the independence that comes with having no plans, wrapping gifts, or attending any holidays.
Travel until you come to a quiet area where you can at last unwind.

Option 4: An Exclusive Yacht in the Heart of Nowhere

This is the way out if you want complete seclusion.
Where: On a lavish yacht in the middle of the ocean, the only "gifts" available are the sun, the sea, and total seclusion.
What's Going to Happen: Sail from one isolated cove to another during the day.
Your holiday décor this year is the beach view, so forget about Christmas trees and lights.
Bring a chef on board who can prepare anything other than Christmas fare (fruitcakes and turkeys are not permitted).
Look up at the stars at night without seeing a single Christmas light.
Allow the world to rejoice in the festive season as you quietly drift off.

Option 5: Deserted Desert Retreat

Although it's snowy around the holidays, what if you could travel to a place where there isn't a chance of snow or festive atmosphere?

Where: Deep in the desert, far from any holiday cheer, lies a peaceful refuge.

What's Going to Happen: Savor the broad, deserted vistas devoid of people, stores, or Christmas lights.

Enjoy lengthy walks in the pleasant weather while keeping in mind that everyone else is engrossed in a holiday frenzy.

Sip on some iced tea while the sun sets over the beach dunes.

Take in the quiet that only the desert can provide; there aren't any "fa-la-la-la-las" here.

After the holidays, come home with a whole new outlook and no idea how much tinsel you missed.

It's Your Turn Now!

Select the location of your dream Christmas getaway. If you could get away from the holidays entirely, where would you go?

Put your escape strategy in writing. How are you going to respond? Why won't you act? When you're not on vacation, how will you pass the time in your paradise?

Shut your eyes and visualize being there. Inhale deeply; there are no holiday stressors, no shopping lists, and no songs.

Bonus Task: Arrange a brief getaway in real life. You might not be able to vanish onto a tropical island, but you can make your own little getaway at home with a few peaceful hours, a nice book, and a strict no-holiday-music policy.

17

Day 17: Holiday Riddles

> **Snarky Quote of the Day:**
>
> "What's more puzzling than holiday plans? These riddles!"

Greetings on Day 17 of the Advent Calendar "I Hate Christmas"!
The holidays may be complicated enough with family get-togethers, mischievous Santas, and trying to remember who is allergic to what. But today, let's put that mayhem aside and focus on something equally confusing: witty festive riddles. Prepare to show off your wit (and snark) with these cheerful but challenging riddles.

Activity:

Complete a set of ironic riddles with a festive theme. You might roll your eyes, sigh, or chuckle at them, but that's all part of the fun! Try your hand at responding to them, or think of some amusingly absurd responses of your own.

Bonus Challenge:
Share one of these riddles with someone else and see if they can figure it out (or groan at the punchline). It's all about spreading the sarcastic holiday cheer!

What do you get when you cross a Christmas tree with an iPhone?
Answer: Pine needles in your screen.

Why did the Christmas cookie go to therapy?
Answer: It had too many layers of emotional baggage (and frosting).

What do reindeer use to clean their sleigh?
Answer: Comet. (Get it? The reindeer... and the cleaning product!)

Why don't Christmas lights ever get along?
Answer: Because they're always getting tangled up in drama.

Why was the Christmas tree so bad at knitting?
Answer: It kept dropping its needles.

What's the difference between a snowman and a holiday shopper?
Answer: One has a nose made of coal, the other is cold and has no nose left after hours of mask-wearing in crowded malls.

Why don't elves play hide and seek?
Answer: Because good luck finding them—they're too short to spot over the wrapping paper piles.

Why was the holiday turkey always so bad at telling jokes?
Answer: It couldn't stop stuffing the punchline.

What did the Grinch say after Christmas dinner?
Answer: "I'm full of holiday spirit... and mashed potatoes."

Why did Santa start taking yoga classes?
Answer: Because he needed to work on his flexibility after squeezing down chimneys all night.

What do you call someone who loves Christmas decorations but hates taking them down?
Answer: A procrastinator with a very festive January.

What do you get when you ask for peace and quiet for Christmas?
Answer: A house full of relatives yelling over each other.

18

Day 18: Anti-Christmas Checklist

> **Snarky Quote of the Day:**
>
> *"The only list I'm making is things I refuse to do."*

Greetings on Day 18 of the Advent Calendar "I Hate Christmas"! Today is all about establishing your anti-Christmas checklist, so forget about making a to-do list. While there are many customs and expectations surrounding the holidays, you're breaking with tradition this year. Which activities this season do you vehemently refuse to engage in? This is your opportunity to make a list of things you're expressing a firm "No" to, whether that means making 200 cookies or pretending to love caroling.

Activity:

Create a list of everything you will not, under any circumstances, do over the holidays. Use your imagination! This is your own list of holiday insubordination; put everything on your "anti-list," including unpleasant customs, stressful occasions, and labor-intensive chores.

Do you need some motivation?
To get you started, here is an example of an anti-Christmas checklist:

The Ultimate Anti-Christmas Checklist

- [ ] **No Baking 200 Cookies** *"Sorry, I'll pass on the sugar coma. I'll be buying cookies instead and calling it a day."*

- [ ] **No Ugly Sweater Parties** *"Wearing something hideous just to fit in? No, thanks. I'll be cozy in my regular, non-ironic sweater."*

- [ ] **No Singing in a Christmas Choir** *"The only time I'm singing is in the shower, and it's definitely not going to be 'Silent Night.'"*

- [ ] **No Over-the-Top Decorations**
"I'm putting up one string of lights. That's it. Maybe."

- [ ] **No Wrapping Gifts with Pinterest-Perfect Bows**
"If it's wrapped in plain paper and has tape stuck everywhere, it's still a gift. Good enough!"

- [ ] **No Forced Holiday Small Talk**
"I refuse to engage in awkward small talk about my 'holiday plans' with people I barely know. The plan is to avoid it."

- [ ] **No Standing in Line for Holiday Sales**
"Fighting over a toaster on sale is not on my holiday wish list. Online shopping only!"

- [ ] **No Hosting Big Family Dinners**
"This year, I'm 'hosting' pizza delivery and a quiet evening. Sorry, Grandma."

- [ ] **No Listening to 'Jingle Bells' on Repeat**
"If I hear it more than once in a day, the headphones are going on. Peace and quiet is my Christmas soundtrack."

- [ ] **No Sending Holiday Cards**
"If you didn't get a card, it's because I didn't send any. Consider it an eco-friendly gesture!"

- [ ] **No Holiday Crafting**
"Glitter? No way. I'm not spending hours making wreaths that end up shedding pine needles everywhere."

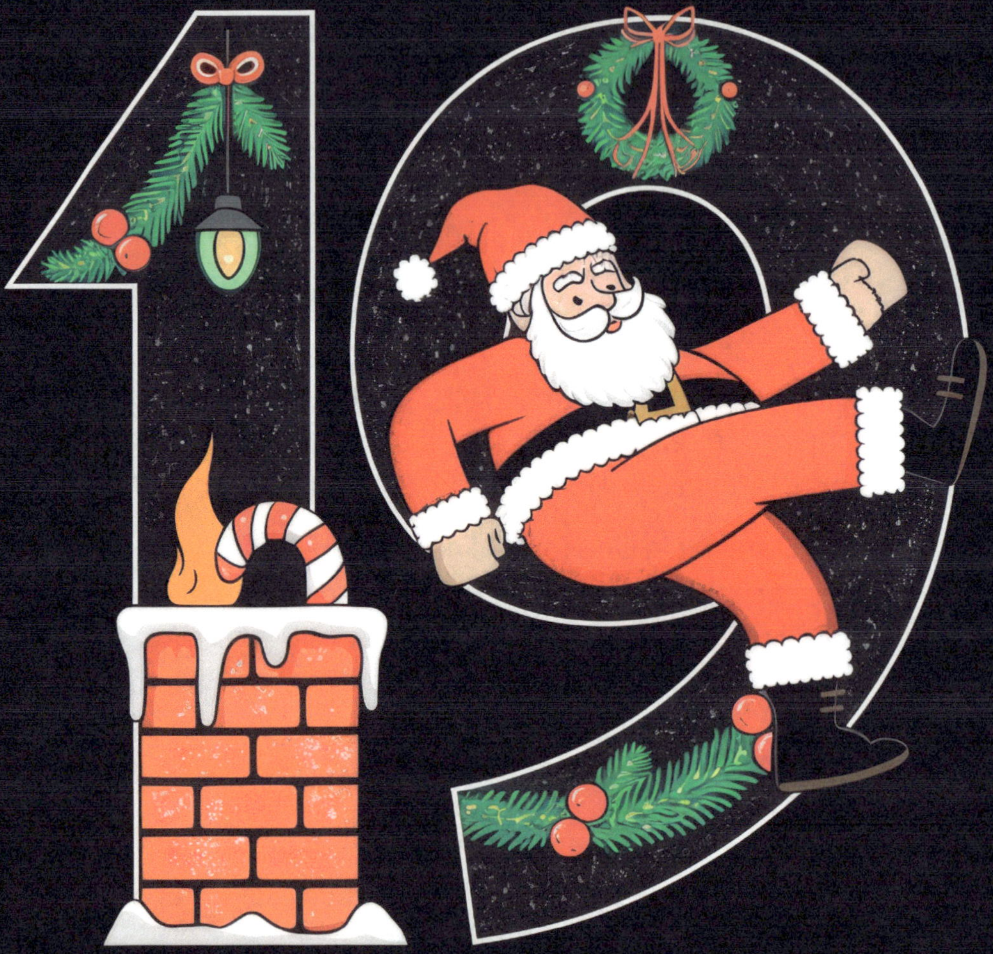

Day 19: Fun Fact: Why Red and Green?

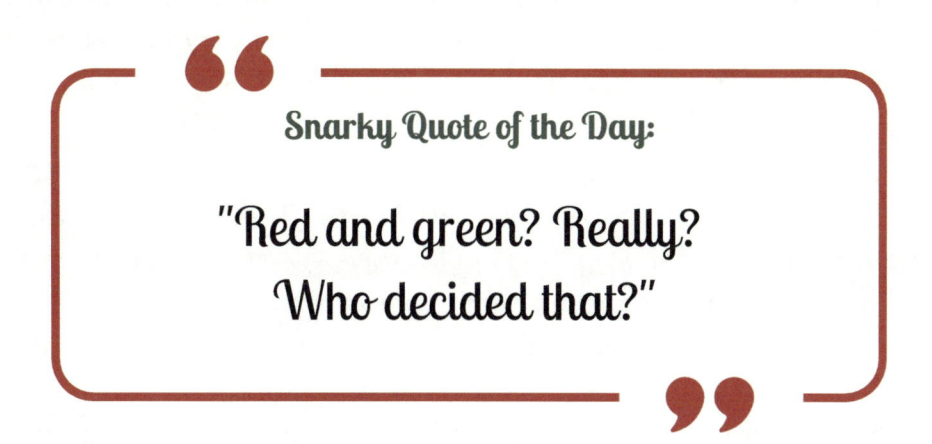

> **Snarky Quote of the Day:**
>
> "Red and green? Really? Who decided that?"

Greetings on Day 19 of the Advent Calendar "I Hate Christmas"! Have you ever wondered why red and green dominate the holiday season? We're delving into the peculiar past of these well-known Christmas hues today. Warning: This story begins with *holly*, you know, the spiky plant that resembles Christmas but will hurt you if you walk too close. How... joyous.

Activity:

Go over the strange history of why red and green were chosen as the official Christmas colors. Then, share this information with someone who is probably not interested in knowing this little known truth but will still find it interesting (because why not).

Fun Fact: Why Red and Green?

Believe it or not, red and green became Christmas colors because of holly—yes, that prickly, evergreen plant that everyone seems to think makes great decoration.

In ancient times, holly was a symbol of protection and good luck. Pagans believed that holly could ward off evil spirits (and possibly your annoying relatives). Since holly stays green even in the dead of winter and has bright red berries, it naturally became associated with the idea of life and fertility during the colder months.

When Christmas traditions started to develop, holly was adopted into Christian symbolism as well. The green leaves were said to represent eternal life, and the red berries were linked to the blood of Christ. And just like that, red and green became the colors of the season. So the next time you're decking the halls, you can thank holly for that festive (and slightly stabby) color scheme.

It's Your Turn Now!

Now It's Your Turn:
- Share this weird fact with someone today.
- Drop it into a conversation like, "Hey, did you know we're all obsessed with red and green because of holly? Because nothing says 'Merry Christmas' like a plant that looks like it wants to fight you."

Bonus Challenge:
The next time you see a house decked out in red and green, casually mention that it's all because of ancient beliefs about holly. Watch as your random trivia knowledge either fascinates or mildly confuses those around you.

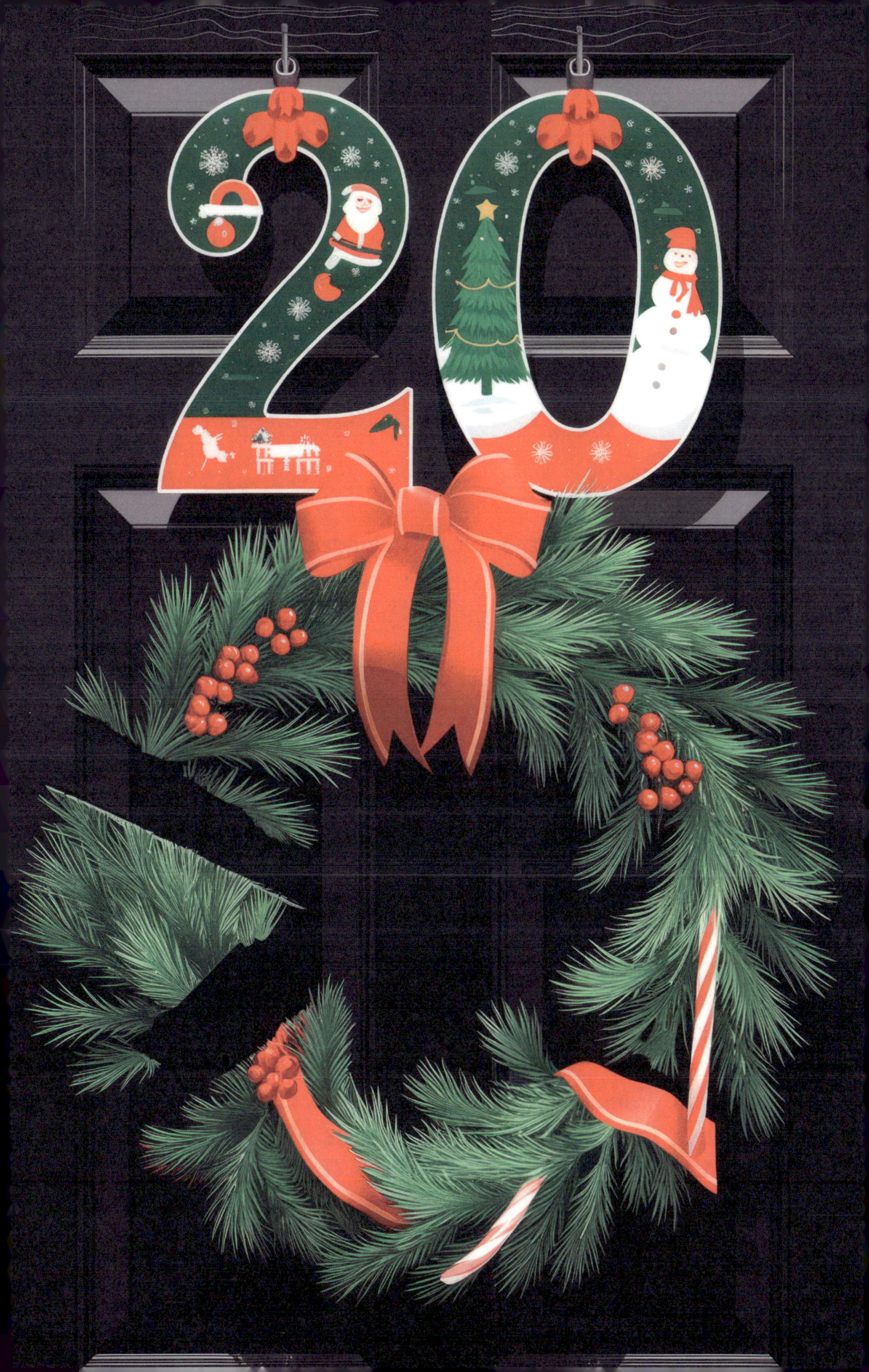
20

Day 20: Sarcastic Gift Tags

> **Snarky Quote of the Day:**
>
> *"This gift is almost as special as you."*

Greetings on Day 19 of the Advent Calendar "I Hate Christmas"! Have you ever wondered why red and green dominate the holiday season? We're delving into the peculiar past of these well-known Christmas hues today. Warning: This story begins with *holly*, you know, the spiky plant that resembles Christmas but will hurt you if you walk too close. How... joyous.

Activity:

Giving gifts is a Christmas custom, but let's face it: occasionally, the excitement of selecting gifts feels more like a burden. So why not play around with it a little bit? Today's project is all about making snarky gift tags, as opposed to the typical sentimental and dull ones. These clever labels will make everyone giggle while revealing the true meaning behind your gifts!

Task: Make ironic gift tags to affix to your Christmas gifts. The objective? Make your tags as sly and cheeky as you can to add a little spice to the gift-giving procedure. Go ahead and use some original sass!

Do you need some motivation?
To get you started, consider these examples of snarky gift tags:

Sarcastic Gift Tags

To: You, because I had to
"Let's be real—I'm only doing this because it's tradition."

From: Someone who didn't want to buy this
"This gift was an afterthought. But hey, it's still wrapped, so there's that."

To: The least annoying person I know
"You should feel honored. Most people didn't even make the gift list."

From: Me, who totally put thought into this
"I definitely didn't buy this last-minute. Nope, not at all."

To: You, but don't get too excited
"Lower your expectations now. Trust me."

From: The person who almost re-gifted this
"You're lucky I didn't just pass this on to someone else. Merry Christmas, I guess."

To: Someone I barely know
"Here's a gift to remind us both that we're socially obligated to exchange presents."

From: Someone who forgot we were doing gifts this year
"You're lucky I found this. Let's pretend I remembered."

To: You, because returning this was too much effort
"Enjoy. Returning it would've been more work than it's worth."

From: Me, but don't expect this every year
"This is a one-time deal. Next year, expect a handshake and a smile."

To: You, who I totally didn't draw in Secret Santa
"Pretend you didn't see the recycled wrapping paper. It's fine."

From: Your favorite person, obviously
"Who else would put this much effort into a gift that's mostly meaningless?"

To: You, because I ran out of better ideas
"This was the least terrible option at the store. You're welcome."

From: Me, but really this was Grandma's idea
"I had nothing to do with this. Complaints go to Grandma."

To: The person who already has everything
"Well, now you have this, too. Congrats."

From: Someone who swears this isn't a re-gift
"You have no proof otherwise."

To: The person who said 'No gifts this year'
"Remember when you said we weren't doing gifts? Guess who ignored that."

Now It's Your Turn!
- Create your own sarcastic gift tags and attach them to your presents this year.
- Whether you're being cheeky about a last-minute buy or making fun of the obligation to exchange gifts, these tags will add a little humor to the holiday madness.

Bonus Challenge:
If you're feeling bold, print these tags and use them on actual gifts. Watch your friends and family laugh (or look slightly confused) as they unwrap your snarky holiday cheer.

21

Day 21: The Grinch Cocktail

> **Snarky Quote of the Day:**
>
> *"When life gives you holiday stress, make a Grinch cocktail."*

Greetings on Day 21 of the Advent Calendar "I Hate Christmas"! The stress level may be reaching a breaking point as the holidays get near. But fear not—the task for today is all about adding a dash of irony to some liquid holiday happiness. Presenting the Grinch Cocktail, the ideal beverage to enjoy while avoiding gift-wrapping or ignoring yet another corny Christmas film.

Activity:

To help you relax from the chaos of the holidays, mix up a Grinch cocktail. It's entertaining, green, and just what you need to embrace your inner Grinch. If you sip it while scowling at your tree, bonus points!

Recipe: The Grinch Cocktail

Ingredients:

- 1 oz Midori (melon liqueur) – for that Grinchy green color.
- 1 oz vodka (because holidays require reinforcements).
- ½ oz lemon juice (to add a little sourness to your sarcastic spirit).
- ½ oz simple syrup (just a touch of fake sweetness).
- Sprite or soda water (for fizz—like all those annoying holiday jingles).
- Maraschino cherry (for a "heart that's two sizes too small").

Instructions:

1. Mix It Up:
    - In a shaker filled with ice, combine Midori, vodka, lemon juice, and simple syrup.
    - Shake it like you're shaking off all that holiday stress.
2. Pour:
    - Strain the mixture into a chilled glass filled with ice.
3. Top Off:
    - Add a splash of Sprite or soda water for a bit of fizz—just enough to feel festive without overdoing it.
4. Garnish with a Cherry:
    - Drop a maraschino cherry into the glass. It's symbolic of the Grinch's tiny heart, but hey, you'll still enjoy it!
5. Sip & Scowl:
    - Drink your Grinch cocktail while giving a disapproving look to all things holiday-related. Whether you're wrapping presents or just pretending to be festive, this cocktail will help you get through the season with a grin (or should we say, a Grinchy grin).

22

Day 22: Anti-Festive Self-Care

> **Snarky Quote of the Day:**
>
> "Sometimes the best way to spread holiday cheer is by ignoring everyone."

Welcome to Day 22 of the "I Hate Christmas" Advent Calendar! The holiday season is all about giving, spending time with loved ones, and... non-stop festivity. But let's face it—sometimes the best way to survive the holidays is to take a break from all the cheer and focus on you. Today's activity is all about anti-festive self-care—because nothing says "self-love" like turning off the Christmas music and pretending the holidays don't exist for a little while.

Activity:

Take 30 minutes just for yourself, and make sure it has absolutely nothing to do with Christmas. No carols, no Christmas movies, no tinsel in sight. This is your time to indulge in something you actually enjoy, free from the overwhelming holiday spirit.

DO NOT DISTURB

How to Indulge in Anti-Festive Self-Care:

IStep 1: Select Your Escape

Select an activity that isn't related to Christmas. Here are some suggestions:
- Watch your preferred non-holiday film or television program. No one is decorating trees or singing carols, regardless of whether it's a sitcom or a crime thriller.
- Curl up with a book that doesn't contain any references to reindeer or mistletoe. Think imagination, mystery, or anything that transports you to an other place.
- Play some music or listen to a podcast that has nothing to do with Christmas happiness or jingles. Jazz? Unknown? Thick metal? You decide, as long as it's not a holiday.

Step 2: Establish a No-Christmas Area

Locate a warm area of your house where the festive season doesn't affect you. No lights that flash, no decorations, and no candles that smell like pine. For the next half hour, this is your haven from the Christmas season.

Step 3: Silence the Distractions

Put on your headphones, turn off any holiday advertising on TV, and block out the outside world. Now is the perfect time to act as though you aren't aware that Christmas music is being played by those nearby. You live in a bubble without holidays.

Step 4: Take Care of Yourself

Without a little indulgence, self-care cannot exist. Get yourself something to eat, drink, or even make yourself some tea or coffee that doesn't taste like candy canes or gingerbread.

Anti-Festive Self-Care Ideas:

Binge Watch a Non-Holiday Show:
"Forget the Christmas movies. I'm watching a true crime documentary marathon. Nothing says 'self-care' like solving mysteries."

Read a Gripping Thriller or Fantasy Novel:
"Let's see… should I read about elves in a snowstorm or dragons in a battle? Dragons it is!"

Take a Long, Non-Holiday Bath:
"No peppermint-scented anything. Just bubbles and silence, please."

Play a Video Game or Puzzle That's Totally Non-Festive:
"If anyone sends me a Candy Crush Christmas level, I'm blocking them."

Do Absolutely Nothing:
"30 minutes of pure nothingness. No wrapping, no baking, no decorating. Just staring at the wall and enjoying the peace."

Now It's Your Turn!
- Take a break from the holiday madness. Set aside 30 minutes today to completely unplug from the season.
- Choose something that has zero festive vibes—something that's purely for you.

Bonus Challenge:
Turn this 30-minute break into a daily routine for the rest of the holidays. Even if it's just 10 minutes a day, giving yourself that small slice of anti-festive time can help you survive the season with your sanity intact.

SANTA'S FUEL

23

Day 23: Bullshit Christmas Tradition

> **Snarky Quote of the Day:**
>
> "Who needs holiday traditions when you can binge-watch TV?"

Greetings on Day 23 of the Advent Calendar "I Hate Christmas"!
We are all aware of how excessive holiday customs may be. It seems like the holiday season is filled with traditions that nobody genuinely loves but everyone pretends to adore, like baking an endless amount of cookies and decorating the tree. The goal of today's exercise is to come up with a crazy Christmas custom that, although seeming festive, is, to be honest, entirely silly.

Activity:

Concoct a "tradition" that, while seemingly joyous, is utterly absurd and incredibly meaningless. Consider the strangest, laziest, or most ridiculous thing you can imagine adopting as a Christmas custom. The better, the more absurd!

Need some inspiration?
Here are a few examples of bullshit Christmas traditions to get your creativity flowing:

Bullshit Christmas Traditions:

The Annual Pretend to Enjoy Fruitcake Day
"It's that special time of year when we all gather around the table, slice up a brick of fruitcake, and pretend it's delicious. Everyone takes one polite bite, nods in fake approval, and quietly spits it out when no one's looking."

The Christmas Gift Wrapping Marathon (with No Gifts)
"Every Christmas Eve, we sit down and wrap random boxes with leftover paper from the previous year. There are no actual gifts inside, but we wrap them anyway and admire how 'festive' they look under the tree. The next morning, we unwrap them just for the sake of it."

The Annual Ugly Ornament Competition
"Each family member is required to make or find the ugliest ornament possible and hang it on the tree. The goal is to make the tree look as hideous as possible. The winner gets a 'trophy' that's just an even uglier ornament for next year."

The Christmas Light Flicker-Off
"We set up all the Christmas lights and then gather around for the grand moment... when we turn them off as fast as possible to save on the electric bill. Whoever can turn them off in record time wins!"

The Silent Gift Exchange
"Instead of explaining what the gift is or why we bought it, we pass out gifts in total silence. No one is allowed to say anything—not even 'thank you.' We just awkwardly nod and move on."

The Christmas Cookie Dunk Contest
"Bake a batch of cookies and then dunk them in whatever drink is nearby. Coffee, hot chocolate, wine—it doesn't matter. The goal is to see how many cookies you can dunk before they completely disintegrate."

The Annual Mismatched Sock Swap
"Everyone brings a single, mismatched sock to swap with someone else. It's a completely useless exchange, but hey, now you have someone else's random sock to add to your pile!"

The Christmas Compliment Competition
"Every year, we gather around and give each other the most over-the-top, ridiculous compliments. 'Your holiday spirit is so strong, it could light up a small country,' or 'That sweater is so amazing, it should be in a museum.' The goal is to be as fake and dramatic as possible."

The Annual Couch Sitting Ceremony
"We all gather around the living room and take turns sitting on the couch, doing absolutely nothing. Each person gets five minutes to 'officially' sit, sigh, and say, 'Well, that was nice.' Then it's the next person's turn."

Now It's Your Turn!
- Create your own bullshit Christmas tradition. What's something absurd that could become a holiday ritual in your world?
- Write it down, make it sound official, and imagine your friends or family actually doing it.

Bonus Challenge:
Share your made-up tradition with a friend or family member and see if they'd be willing to give it a try. Who knows? You might accidentally start a real tradition that everyone loves… or hates!

24

Merry crisis.

Day 24: Christmas Eve Survival Kit

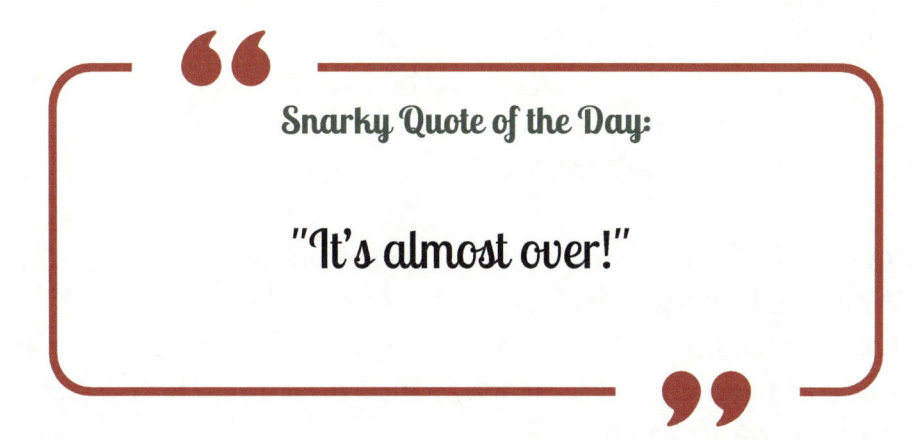

> **Snarky Quote of the Day:**
>
> *"It's almost over!"*

Greetings on Day 24 of the Advent Calendar "I Hate Christmas"! Christmas Eve has arrived, and you can now see the finish line. You must make it through the last stretch of the holiday chaos before you can formally bid it farewell. The goal of today's task is to put together the essential supplies for your ultimate Christmas Eve survival kit—the things you'll need to survive the final moments of the holiday madness without losing your mind.

Activity:

Assemble a survival kit for Christmas Eve so you can maintain your composure while everyone else is enjoying the festivities. This kit will include everything you need to get through the evening, whether you're avoiding family get-togethers, avoiding the last-minute gift rush, or just trying to escape the Christmas mood.

The Ultimate Survival Kit for Christmas Eve

Noise-Canceling Headphones:
"Because if I hear one more Christmas carol, I'm going to lose it." Shut out the holiday bustle and withdraw into your own peaceful bubble. Either enjoy the silence or play your favorite music that has nothing to do with the holidays.

Your Go-To Snacks (That Aren't Festive, Naturally)
"Who needs gingerbread cookies when I've got nachos?" Make sure to stock up on your favorite non-Christmas foods. These are your go-to comfort foods—chips, popcorn, or an enormous tub of ice cream, for example.

A List of Marathon-Watchable Non-Holiday Films
"It's time to stop watching Christmas movies. I'm watching something that involves dragons or explosions." Make a list of all the shows or movies that aren't related to the holidays at all. Consider watching comedy, thrillers, action movies, or even a nature program to divert your attention from the season.

A Warm Blanket (devoid of Holiday Themes)
"It's just a blanket, not a symbol of 'holiday warmth.'" Put on a warm, comfortable blanket and act as though you're going to hibernate until January. If it's the softest item you own without any reindeer or snowflakes on it, bonus points.

A Novel That Has Nothing to Do with Christmas
"I'm taking a trip to a place where nobody is hanging up the lights." Select a decent book to curl up with and do something completely different from holiday happiness. Make sure the book transports you far, far away from Christmas, whether it's an epic fantasy or a nail-biting thriller.

A Selection of Drinks
"Eggnog? Thank you not at all. I'm having a cocktail, tea, or wine." Pour yourself a glass of your preferred non-festival alcohol. This is the time for you to relax and get away from the chaos of the holidays, whether it's with a big mug of tea, a sophisticated cocktail, or a bottle of wine.

Do Not Disturb sign
"If anyone needs me, they'll have to get through this door first," reads a "Do Not Disturb" sign. Put a "Do Not Disturb" sign on your door, or just give your family a strange look. This indication formalizes that you deserve some time to yourself.

A playlist against Christmas
"Carrols are not permitted. simply songs that I genuinely enjoy." Make a playlist with all of your favorite songs that don't even somewhat relate to the holidays. Regardless of your musical tastes —classical, pop, or rock—make sure there are no carols playing.

Putting the phone in airplane mode
"No texts, no calls, no last-minute holiday emergencies." To avoid last-minute texts about holiday plans or gift inquiries, put your phone on airplane mode or simply turn it off. It's time for you to switch off.

A Candle (Without A Christmasy Scent)
"Neither pine nor cinnamon. Just a lovely, soothing aroma." Light a candle that doesn't have a Christmas scent. Choose a relaxing aroma, such as lavender or vanilla, and let the calming effect to aid in your relaxation.

It's Your Turn Now!

Prepare yourself for a stress-free evening by gathering the supplies for your Christmas Eve survival kit.
When everyone else is busy wrapping presents and decorating for the holidays, use the kit to create your own small haven away from the hustle and bustle.

Bonus Task: Include something personally meaningful in your survival pack! Perhaps it's a stand-up comedy playlist, your all-time favorite board game, or a handmade product. Include anything that helps you relax in your getaway strategy.

And never forget that the goal is almost here! You'll make it through Christmas Eve with your survival gear in hand, and you'll emerge prepared to face the new year (ideally with a lot less stress). **Cheers to surviving!**

Ending: You Survived... Barely

> **Snarky Quote:**
> "Congratulations, you've successfully avoided most of the holiday chaos. That's a win, right?"

You succeeded. You've made it to the end of the 'I Hate Christmas' Advent Calendar, which has taken 24 days of avoiding seasonal cheer, making ironic gift tags, drinking Grinch cocktails, and creating absurd customs.

Perhaps you've avoided some of the biggest holiday transgressions, or perhaps you've simply become adept at quietly rolling your eyes while feigning enjoyment of particular customs. In any case, you merit a respite. You've vented, you've laughed, and you've managed to make the holidays much more sardonic and a bit less stressful.

How Now?
The good news is that it will soon come to an end. The decorations will come down, the Christmas carols will eventually become less noticeable, and the pressure to celebrate will eventually vanish. You can get back to your regular life without having to deal with mall Santas, mistletoe, and tinsel all the time. But before you put this book down and go straight into your post-holiday hibernation, stop and consider what the true lesson is of this:

To get through the holidays, you don't have to adore them.
If you would rather to curl up under a blanket with a wonderful non-holiday novel, you don't have to be carried up by the spirit of things. It's not necessary for you to attend parties, bake cookies, or force a grin when you'd rather not. That's alright, too.

The goal of this advent calendar was to survive the season without losing your sense of humor, wit, or sarcasm. You've mastered the art of the anti-Christmas if you can find delight in saying "No" to the mayhem, roll your eyes at the clichés, and chuckle through the stress.

Final Thought: Having made it this far, you may even find yourself giggling at some of the absurdity of it all. Perhaps you'll come up with even more ridiculous customs, send Santa even more sarcastic letters, and assemble an even larger survival pack the next year. Perhaps you will choose to simply avoid the season altogether, and that is also acceptable.

Whatever your approach to the holidays may be going forward, never forget that you are the Grinch of your own tale, and that's something to be happy about.

Now go ahead and celebrate that you survived another holiday season by taking a big breath and sipping on your final Grinch beverage. You made it through. And that is something to raise a glass to.

Until Next Year, Keep Calm and Stay Sarcastic.

Manufactured by Amazon.ca
Bolton, ON